I Took the Moon for a Walk

Written by Carolyn Curtis

Illustrated by Alison Jay

Barefoot Books
Celebrating Art and Story

I took the Moon for a walk last night.

It followed behind like a still summer kite,

Though there wasn't a string or a tail in sight

when I took the Moon for a walk.

I carried my blue torch just in case

the Moon got scared and hid its face.

But it peeked through clouds
that were fragile as lace
When I took the Moon for
a walk.

I warned the Moon to rise a bit higher

so it wouldn't get hooked on a church's tall spire,

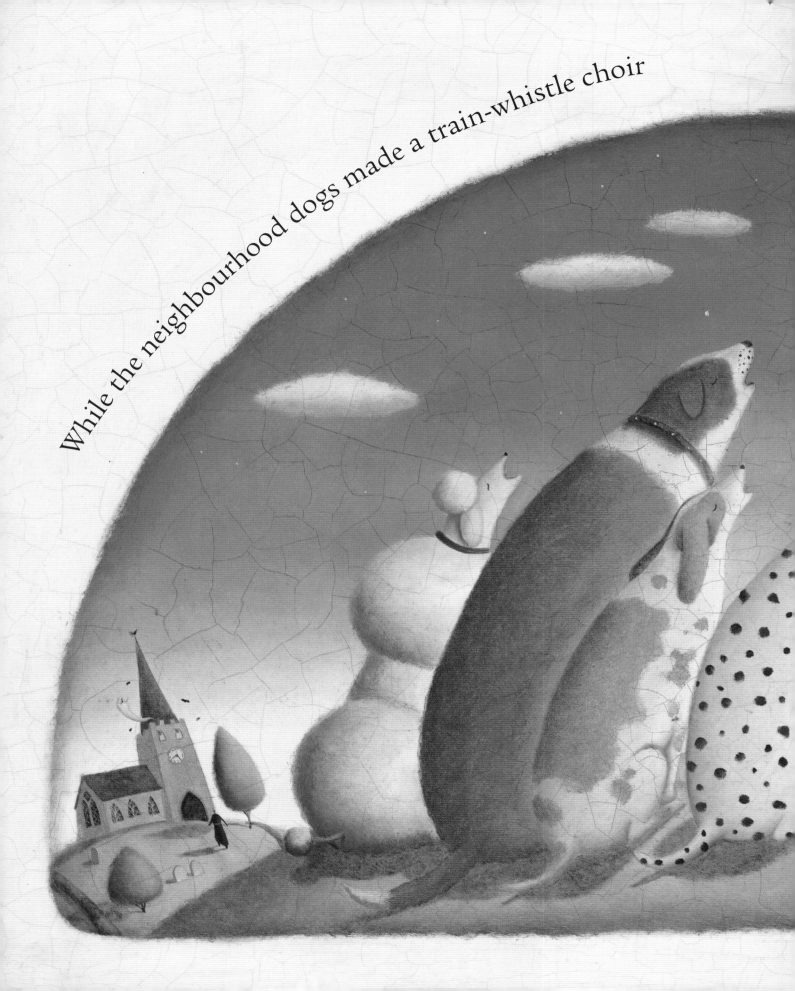

While the neighbourhood dogs made a train-whistle choir

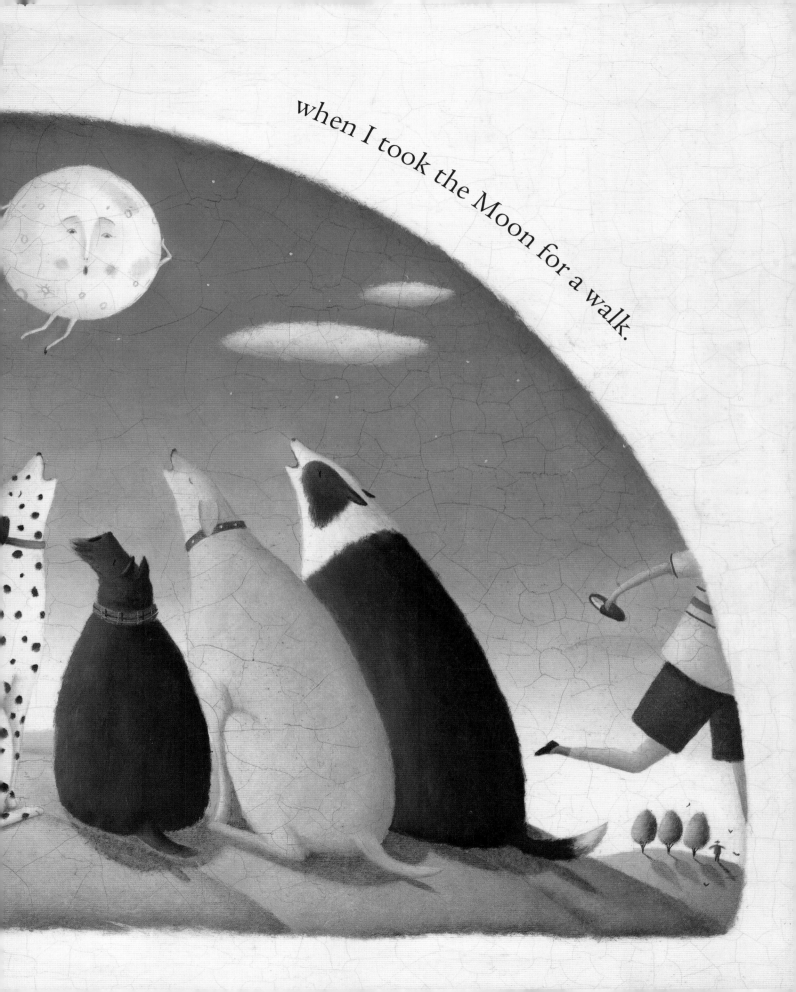

when I took the Moon for a walk.

We tiptoed through grass where the night crawlers creep

when the rust-bellied robins have all gone to sleep,

And the Moon called the dew so the grass seemed to weep
When I took the Moon for a walk.

We raced for the swings,
where I kicked my feet high
And imagined the Moon had
just asked me to fly,

Hand holding hand through the starry night sky

when I took the Moon for a walk.

We danced 'cross the bridge where the smooth waters flow.

The Moon was above and the Moon was below,

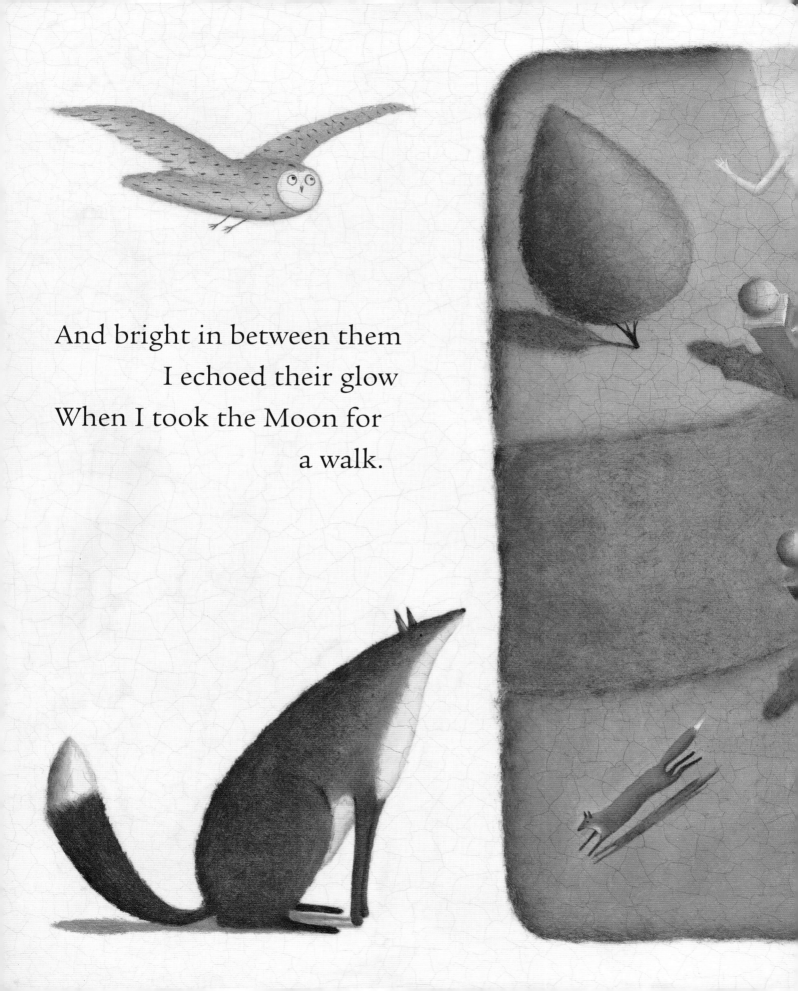

And bright in between them
I echoed their glow
When I took the Moon for
a walk.

Then as we turned back, the Moon kept me in sight.

It followed me home and stayed there all night,

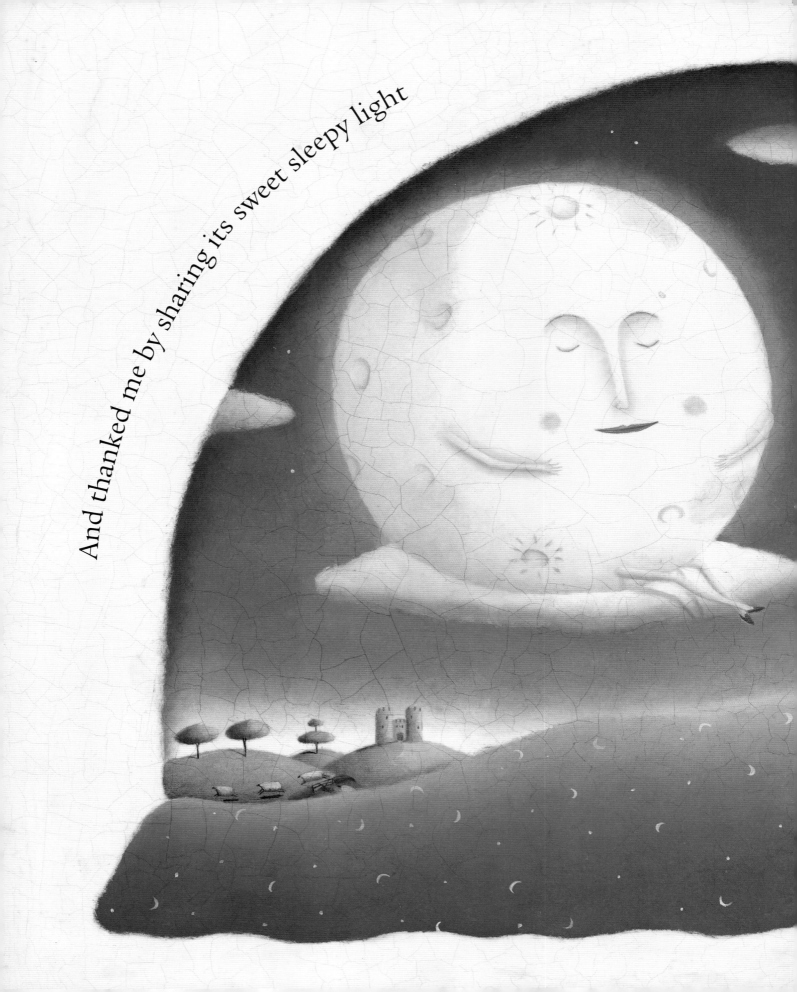

And thanked me by sharing its sweet sleepy light

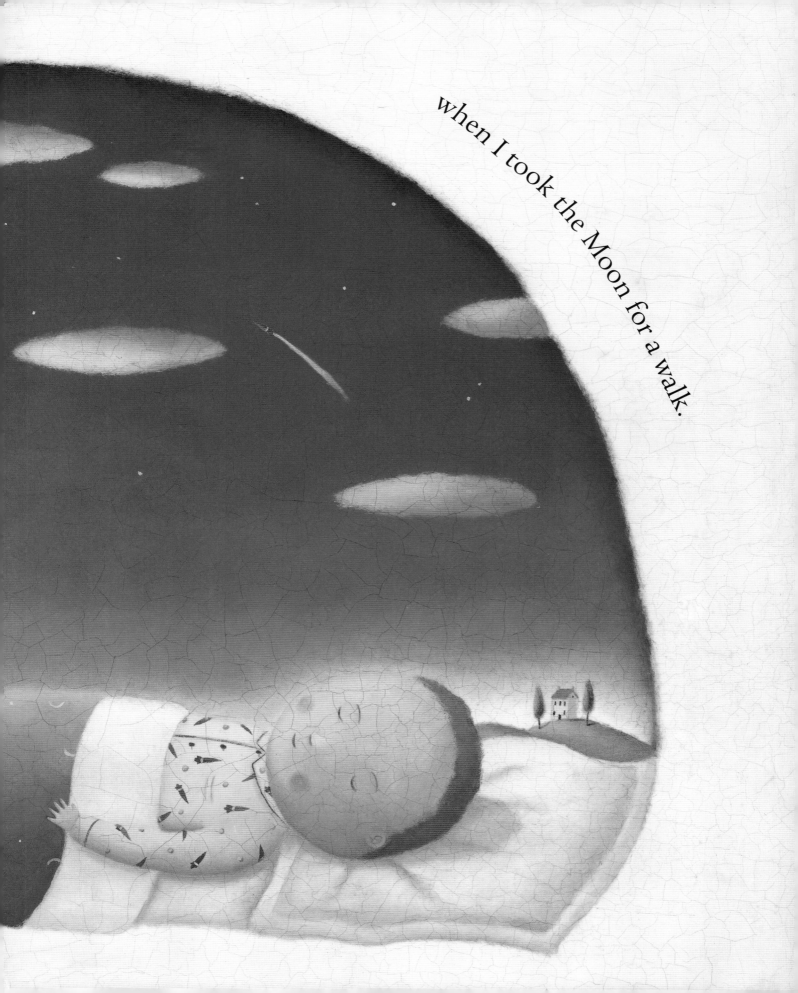

when I took the Moon for a walk.

The Mysterious Moon

What do you see when you look at the moon? Children who live in Europe and the United States imagine that they see a man when they look at the moon. Children in Japan and India see a rabbit, and children in Australia see a kitten. But all children, no matter where they live, look up in wonder at the same moon.

The moon is primarily made of rock with a small iron core. It creates no light of its own, but reflects sunlight.

The shape of the moon seems to change during the month because the sunlight strikes the moon at different angles as it travels through space. These shapes are called 'phases'. Here are some of the phases of the moon:

New Moon   *Crescent Moon*   *Half Moon*   *Gibbous Moon*   *Full Moon*

When the moon is growing larger in the sky, we say that it is 'waxing'. When it is growing smaller, we say that it is 'waning'.

For people all over the world, the moon has always been an important way to measure time. Although the solar calendar has become the standard international way of doing this, many people still use lunar, or moon, calendars.

The moon can be a friend to farmers and gardeners — those who follow tradition know that the best time to sow seeds and transplant young shoots is when the moon is waxing.

Moon festivals are celebrated in many societies. The Chinese Moon Festival is held during the Harvest Moon — the full moon that rises in mid-autumn.

Many Celtic and Native American festivals are also held at the time of the Harvest Moon, when the people give thanks for the harvest and for all living things on earth.

The World at Night

If you took the moon for a walk through your neighbourhood, what would you show it? What would you hear, and what would you see?

Wherever you are, you would probably see some nocturnal creatures — mammals, birds and insects that usually sleep during the day and come out to hunt and eat at night. They are especially adapted to life under the moon and stars:

Cats have eyes that see very well in the dark.

Rabbits have large ears that capture sound across long distances.

Bats use sounds and echoes to help them fly safely and find food.

Fireflies light up at night so that they can find each other.

Owls have necks that can turn right around and huge, flat eyes that enable them to see other creatures that are far away.

Some flowers are nocturnal too. They bloom and release their fragrance after dark.

And although you are asleep during the night, your mind is not! During the day, your waking, or conscious, mind is active, but when you sleep, your dreaming, or unconscious, mind is busy. So, the world at night is not as quiet as it seems!

For my nephew Christopher, *who first walked the Moon*
and my mother Estella, *who held his hand*
For my father Harold, *the Star we steer by*
and Lucan, *my Sun*
and, of course, for Emilie, *for Everything* — C. C.

The author extends heartfelt thanks to the Society of Children's Book Writers and Illustrators for generous support in the form of a
Barbara Karlin Grant, WarmLines Parent Resources, Jane Yolen, the Jeff Kelly and Newton Library Critique Groups, and Alison Keehn.

For Mark, happy moon walking, love from Alison.

Barefoot Books
124 Walcot Street
Bath
BA1 5BG

This book was typeset in 22pt Legacy Serif Book
The illustrations were prepared in alkyd oil paint on paper with a crackling varnish

Colour separation by Bright Arts, Singapore
Printed and bound in Singapore by Tien Wah Press (Pte) Ltd

This book has been printed on 100% acid-free paper

ISBN 1-84148-602-7

British Cataloguing-in-Publication Data: a catalogue
record for this book is available from the British library

1 3 5 7 9 8 6 4 2

Barefoot Books
Celebrating Art and Story

At Barefoot Books, we celebrate art and story
with books that open the hearts and minds of children
from all walks of life, inspiring them to read deeper,
search further, and explore their own creative gifts.
Taking our inspiration from many different cultures,
we focus on themes that encourage independence of
spirit, enthusiasm for learning, and acceptance of other
traditions. Thoughtfully prepared by writers, artists and
storytellers from all over the world, our products combine
the best of the present with the best of the past to educate
our children as the caretakers of tomorrow.

www.barefootbooks.com